Llyfrgelloedd Caerdydd
www.caerdy
Cardiff L
www.cardiff.gov.uk/libraries

CAERDYDD
CARDIFF

KT-165-017

JASON BANKS and the PUMPKIN of DOOM

ACC. No: 07027092

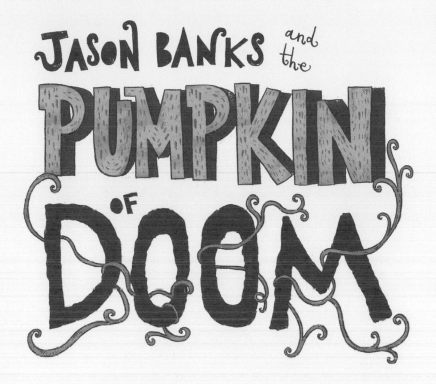

Jason Banks and the Pumpkin of Doom

Gillian Cross

ILLUSTRATED BY
Sarah Horne

Barrington Stoke

First published in 2018 in Great Britain by
Barrington Stoke Ltd
18 Walker Street, Edinburgh, EH3 7LP

www.barringtonstoke.co.uk

Text © 2018 Gillian Cross
Illustrations © 2018 Sarah Horne

The moral right of Gillian Cross and Sarah Horne to be
identified as the author and illustrator of this work has been
asserted in accordance with the Copyright, Designs and
Patents Act, 1988

All rights reserved. No part of this publication may be
reproduced in whole or in any part in any form without the
written permission of the publisher

A CIP catalogue record for this book is available
from the British Library upon request

ISBN: 978-1-78112-813-8

Printed in China by Leo

Contents

Chapter 1
King of the School

Jason Banks was tall and strong, like a superhero. But he wasn't a hero at all.

He was a bully.

Everyone in his class was afraid of him. He pinched the girls and stuck chewing gum in their hair. He hit the boys and stole their lunch money. He laughed at the kids who found school work hard – and he made the clever kids do his homework for him.

Everyone was too scared to tell. So the teachers thought Jason was wonderful. He got full marks in Maths – because no one dared to say he was copying. He wrote amazing stories – because he stole other people's ideas. And he was the top goal-scorer in every game of football before, during and after school.

Because it's easy to score if the goal-keeper's afraid of you.

Jason felt as if he was the king of the school.

One day he walked into class and saw a new girl on the other side of the room. She was small and pale, with red hair and a pointed nose. All the other girls were crowding round her, telling her about the school – about the kids and the teachers and all the little tricks that make life easier. When they saw Jason, they whispered, "That's Jason Banks. Stay away from him. He's mean."

The new girl looked across the room. "Hi, Jason!" she said, "I'm Millie." And she *smiled*. As if she wasn't scared at all.

Jason glared and walked over to the table where she was standing. "Is that your pencil case?" he growled.

The new girl nodded and Jason threw the pencil case on to the floor. When she bent down to pick it up, he pushed her over. She fell on the floor and banged her head on the table leg.

"*Sorry!*" Jason said with a big grin.

"You see?" the other girls whispered. "Jason's *mean*! Stay away from him."

The new girl got up. She didn't say a word. She brushed the dust off her clothes and put her pencil case back on the table. Then she sat down, with her back to Jason.

She didn't look at him for the rest of the day. Not once.

That's fixed her! Jason thought as he walked home at the end of the day. *She knows I'm the king of the school. And tomorrow is going to be even better!*

But he was wrong about that.

*

When Jason woke up the next morning, the house was empty. As always. His mum always went off to work before he was awake.

He got dressed and ate a packet of biscuits for breakfast. Then he put on his coat, opened the front door – and stopped. Because there was something outside the door, blocking his way. Something very strange.

A pumpkin.

It was bright orange. And huge. And it had an ugly face painted on the front, with staring eyes and big sharp teeth. Propped up on top of it was a notice:

I AM THE PUMPKIN OF DOOM.

Jason stared. Where had it come from? Was it a joke? Was someone watching, to see if he was scared? Huh! He was Jason Banks and he wasn't afraid of anything!

"Stupid pumpkin!" he said out loud. "Get out of my way!"

He took a step back and kicked as hard as he could. "GOAL!" he shouted as his foot crashed into the pumpkin.

But the pumpkin didn't move. Not a centimetre. Jason's foot thudded against its bright orange skin and he gave a huge yell.

"OWWW!"

It was like smashing his foot against a rock. Like kicking a cliff. It hurt!

"OWWWW!" Jason yelled, hopping around on one leg. How could a pumpkin do that? Why was it so heavy?

He bent down to look. The pumpkin's top was loose, like a lid. He lifted it off. Inside, the pumpkin was hollow – and filled with big stones.

That was why his foot hurt so much. He really *had* kicked a rock.

"Stupid pumpkin!" he shouted again. But he couldn't stop his voice wobbling.

Then he heard a funny little noise. When he looked up, he saw a girl with a bike. She had stopped, right outside his house, and she was staring into his garden. A small pale girl, with red hair and a pointed nose.

Jason knew he'd seen her before, but he couldn't remember where. His foot was hurting so much he couldn't think properly.

"What are you staring at?" he yelled. "Push off!"

He wanted to give her a real push. But when he took a step towards her – OUCH!! His foot hurt! He had to bend down and rub it to make it feel better.

When he looked up, the girl had gone.

*

Somehow, Jason limped to school. He was very slow and he only just got there in time. When he walked into his classroom, the first person he saw was the pale girl with the pointed nose.

Oh no! Now he remembered her. She was Millie, the new girl – and she'd seen

him yelling and hopping around on one leg.
Looking like an idiot.

Bet she's told the whole class, he thought.
They're all going to laugh at me. He glared
round the room, waiting for the first giggle.
He felt angry with everyone there.

But no one laughed. No one even looked at
him – except the new girl. She glanced across
the room and gave him a tiny little grin. As if
she was saying, *Don't worry. I won't tell.*

Jason couldn't believe it. He was so
surprised that he forgot about the pumpkin
for a moment.

But not for long. He spent the rest of
the day thinking about it. Where had that
pumpkin come from? Who had put it there?

And *why*?

*

When Jason got home after school, the pumpkin had vanished. But Jason couldn't forget it. His foot was still sore. And when he took off his sock, the big toenail was black.

He was furious. Someone had put that pumpkin there on purpose. As a trap. When he found out who, that person was going to be very sorry. No one got away with playing tricks on Jason Banks!

Chapter 2
The Second Pumpkin

The next morning, the pumpkin was there again. Exactly the same. Round and orange and huge, with a big notice on top.

I AM THE PUMPKIN OF DOOM.

Jason saw it as soon as he opened the front door. He glared at it and looked around to see if anyone was watching. He couldn't see anyone, but he shouted anyway.

"I'm not a fool!" he yelled. He marched up to the pumpkin and grabbed its lid. "You can't trick me like that again. I KNOW there's a rock in here!"

He snatched the lid off the pumpkin and bent over to look inside.

He was wrong about the rock. This time, it wasn't a rock inside the pumpkin. It was a big strong spring – with a boxing glove fixed to the top. When he lifted the lid, the spring bounced up and the boxing glove hit him on the nose. Very hard.

"YOWWWW!" he yelled.

"Oh dear," said a quiet voice from outside the garden. "You poor thing. I bet that hurt."

It was Millie, the new girl, again. She got off her bike and propped it against the hedge. Jason glared at her.

"Go away!" he shouted.

"Your nose is bleeding," Millie said. "And there's blood all over your shirt."

Jason looked down. She was right. Blood was dripping out of his nose and the front of his shirt was bright red. What was he going to do?

"You can't go to school like that," Millie said. "You need a clean shirt."

"I haven't *got* a clean shirt," Jason said. His mum only did the washing once a week. All his other shirts were dirty.

Millie frowned and bit her lip. Then she grinned at Jason. "I know!" she said. "Don't go away. I'll be right back!" She turned her bike round, jumped on and pedalled off, going back the way she'd come.

Jason waited. What else could he do? He couldn't go to school with blood all over his shirt. But he couldn't just stay at home. If his mum found out he'd missed school, she would be cross. Very VERY cross.

He glared down at the pumpkin. "I don't know who put you here," he said to it. "But they're going to be sorry when I find out."

He gave the pumpkin a huge kick and it shot across the garden and thudded against the dustbin. *That's the best place for it!* Jason thought. He ran over and picked it up. He lifted up the dustbin lid, then he threw the pumpkin into the bin. It crashed to the bottom and broke in half.

"Good!" Jason muttered. "That's the end of you."

Then he heard some of the other kids coming down the road, on their way to school. Oh no! He couldn't let them see him with blood all over his shirt. He hid behind the hedge until they had gone past.

Where was that girl? Was she really going to come back?

It was almost ten minutes before he heard her cycling back down the road. She propped her bike against the hedge again and raced into the garden. In her hand was a clean white shirt.

"You can – borrow this," she panted. "It's – my brother's."

Jason grabbed the clean shirt and ran back into the house. He took off the blood-stained shirt, dropped it into the washing basket and put on the clean one. It fitted perfectly.

"Hurry up!" Millie called from outside. "We'll be late if we don't hurry!"

Jason picked up his bag and raced out of the house. "I'll run," he said.

Millie grabbed her bike. She was just going to cycle off when she looked down and groaned. "Oh no!" she said. "I've got a puncture! I'll have to push the bike."

"Bad luck," Jason said.

He raced off and left Millie standing on the pavement. He couldn't wait for her. His mum would be angry if he was late for school.

He ran all the way to school and just made it. The bell was ringing as he went through the school gate and he glanced back down the road to see where Millie was.

She was still a long way off. She was trying to run, but pushing the bike slowed her down. She was going to be at least five minutes late.

That's her *problem*, Jason thought. He turned his back and hurried into school with the rest of his class.

It was ten minutes after the bell when Millie finally walked into the classroom. Mr Jackson, the teacher, frowned and shook his head at her. "You're very late," he said. "What happened?"

"Sorry," Millie muttered. She looked across the room, at Jason. As if she was waiting for him to say something.

Jason opened his mouth. And then shut it again. He could have said that Millie was late because she'd been helping him. But what if Mr Jackson asked why? Then Jason would have to say his nose was bleeding   because he'd been punched by a *pumpkin*.

He couldn't do that.

Millie stared at him, but she didn't say anything.

Mr Jackson frowned. "Come on, Millie. Why weren't you here on time?"

"I – um –" Millie looked down at her hands. "I didn't get up when my alarm went off," she muttered.

Mr Jackson shook his head at her. "That's not good enough," he said. "I'll have to mark you late. If you do it again, the Head will write to your parents."

Millie bit her lip, but she didn't say anything. And she didn't look at Jason again.

Chapter 3
Jason Banks is Scared

When Jason's mum came home that evening, she saw his shirt in the washing basket – and she thought he'd been fighting.

"I've told you to stay out of trouble!" she yelled. "It'll take hours to get the stains out of that shirt. And I'll have to wash the one you borrowed tonight. As if I didn't have enough to do ..." She was very cross.

Jason didn't explain about the pumpkin. He didn't think his mum would believe him. And it made him feel silly. He just muttered "Sorry" and went off to do his homework.

His mum washed and ironed the shirt Millie had lent him. In the morning, she left it on the kitchen table. Jason got ready for school and put the shirt into his bag. Then he opened the front door, just a crack, and looked out into the garden.

No pumpkin.

The garden path was empty.

Jason relaxed. "Of course it's not there," he thought. "I put it in the dustbin. And it broke in half. It's gone." He picked up his bag and stepped into the garden. Everything was OK again.

But – maybe he'd take one last look at the stupid pumpkin. Just to be sure. He shut the front door, went over to the dustbin and lifted the lid.

The dustbin was empty.

THUMP! went Jason's heart. That was impossible. The pumpkin had to be in the dustbin. It couldn't get out on its own.

Could it?

For a moment, he felt afraid. But that was silly. There had to be a sensible reason why the bin was empty. Maybe the bin lorry had collected the rubbish yesterday.

He slammed down the dustbin lid, picked up his bag and walked out of the garden.

And there was the pumpkin.

Not in the bin. Not broken in half. It was standing right in the middle of the pavement. And it was exactly the same as before. Huge and orange and as good as new.

All the other kids would see it on their way to school. They would read the notice on top and spend the rest of the day talking about it.

I AM THE PUMPKIN OF DOOM

Jason shivered. *It can't be there*, he thought. *It's impossible*.

But it was there. Right in the middle of the pavement. Staring at him with its black painted eyes.

It can't be real, Jason thought. *I must be seeing things*. He walked round the pumpkin but he was careful not to touch it. He didn't even look at it. It wasn't going to trick him again.

Once he was past the pumpkin, he went on down the road without turning round. But he hadn't gone far when he heard a voice calling from behind him.

"Jason! Stop! Look!!"

It was that girl again. Millie. She was standing beside the pumpkin, with her bike. And she was pointing at something. "Look at this!" she shouted. "Look what it says on the back!"

So Millie could see the pumpkin too. So it was really there. Jason shivered and walked back up the road to see what Millie was pointing at.

For the first time, he noticed the black words painted across the back of the pumpkin.

JASON BANKS IS SCARED OF ME

Oh no! All the other kids would see it on their way to school. *Jason Banks is scared of me.*

Jason couldn't let that happen. He bent down to grab the pumpkin. It was so big

that his arms only just reached round it. He
picked it up and took it back into his garden.
It was hard to carry and he had to hold it tight
against his chest.

"Hey, you! Millie!" he shouted. "Come and
open the dustbin!"

Millie ran into the garden and lifted the
dustbin lid.

"DIE, pumpkin!" Jason yelled. He threw it
into the bin, as hard as he could. It hit the
bottom with a juicy SQUELCH! and smashed
into dozens of pieces. Jason stepped back and
took a long deep breath.

"That's got rid of that!" he said. "Do you
think any of the other kids saw it?"

Millie shook her head. "I don't think so,"
she said. "It's still very early." Then she
looked down at Jason's shirt – and gasped. "Oh
no! Look!"

JASON BANKS IS SCARED

Jason looked. There were big black marks all over the front of his shirt. They were like letters, but he couldn't quite read them.

"What is it?" he muttered.

Millie frowned. "The paint's come off the pumpkin and gone onto your shirt," she said. "Only, the words are back to front."

"What do you mean?" Jason said. "What does it say?"

Millie stared at the shirt. "It says – um –" She looked up at Jason. She didn't want to tell him.

"*Tell* me!" Jason said, almost shouting. "What does it say?"

Millie gulped. "It says, JASON BANKS IS SCARED. It's backwards, but it's easy to read."

Jason shuddered. "I can't go to school like that. And my mum's going to be furious. She was very angry about the blood on my other shirt. She thought I'd been fighting."

Millie looked puzzled. "Didn't you tell her about the pumpkin?"

"She'd think I was stupid," Jason muttered.

"Well ... you could wash the shirt yourself," Millie said.

"Mum would know," said Jason.

Millie looked at his face. Then she looked at the shirt. "I could wash it for you," she said. "I'll take it home and bring it back tomorrow."

"You?" Jason stared at her. "Why would you wash my shirt?"

Millie grinned. "I like helping people," she said. "Especially my friends."

Friends? Did she think they were friends? Jason didn't know what to say.

"Come on," Millie said. "Or we'll be late for school. You need a clean shirt. Fast."

Jason remembered the shirt in his bag. He pulled it out and looked at Millie. "Is it OK if I wear your brother's shirt again?"

"Of course it is," Millie said. "Just hurry."

Jason changed, very fast, and Millie put the dirty shirt in her bag.

"Right!" she said. "Let's go!" She started walking up the road, pushing her bike. "Come on, Jason."

Jason stared at her. How come she was bossing him about? He was the king of the school and she was a small new girl with a pointed nose. For a second, he started to feel angry.

Then he remembered he was wearing her brother's shirt.

And she was going to wash the paint out of *his* shirt.

And she hadn't told anyone about the pumpkin yesterday.

Millie looked back at him. "Get a move on, Jason Banks! Or do you want to be late?"

Jason ran to catch her up.

Chapter 4
Don't Talk to HIM!

By the time they got to school, there were lots of people in the playground. When other girls saw Millie with Jason, they shouted to her.

"No, Millie! Keep away from Jason!"

"He's horrible!"

"Come over here!"

Millie shook her head and looked at Jason. "They're really mean about you," she whispered as they walked into class. "But it's OK. Don't be scared."

"I'm not scared," Jason said crossly. "They're the ones who are scared. Everyone's –"

Everyone's scared of ME, he was going to say. But he stopped himself. What would Millie think if she knew he liked scaring people?

Would she think *he* was mean?

He didn't say anything else. And he didn't push anyone over all day. Or pull the girls' hair. Or copy anyone's homework. He just sat in his place, at the back of the class, and did a lot of thinking.

*

Jason didn't know if Millie would wait for him at the end of school. She didn't. She left very quickly, all on her own. Jason saw her cycle away. Before he was even out of the school gate, she had gone.

So he walked back from school on his own, the way he did every day.

When he got home, he opened the front door and there was a pile of letters lying on the mat. On top was an envelope and it said:

To Jason's mother

Jason went cold. Who was writing to his mum? Was someone complaining about him? Were they telling her that he was mean to the other kids?

He stared at the letter. He wished he could open it to see who it was from. But he didn't dare. If his mum found out he'd opened one of her letters, he would be in trouble.

He picked the letter up and put it on the table by the door. Everything under it was junk mail and he knew his mum wouldn't want that. She liked him to throw it away, so he picked it up and took it outside to the dustbin.

He wasn't even thinking about the pumpkin that he'd thrown there in the morning.

Not until he lifted the lid. Then he remembered all right.

Because the pumpkin wasn't there. It had vanished. Again.

Jason shivered as he dropped the junk mail into the bin. He didn't feel like the king of the school now. He didn't feel like the king of anything. He felt scared.

How can a pumpkin keep vanishing and coming back? he thought as he went into the house again.

What would the next pumpkin do to him?

And what was in that letter?

He wished he had someone to talk to. Like Millie. He kept looking out of the window, just in case she was cycling past, but the street was empty. And there was no one else about.

*

It seemed a long time until his mum came home. Jason did his homework and ate three peanut butter sandwiches and two bananas, but she still wasn't there. In the end, he turned on the TV, but it was a silly show about some kids in a dance class and he didn't really watch it.

For a start, he was much too worried.

At last he heard his mum's car pull up to the house. Then her key slid into the lock and she opened the front door.

"Hi, Jason," she called. "Have you had a good day?"

"It was OK," Jason muttered.

There was a thud as his mum put her bag down. "What's this?" she said. "A letter?"

Jason heard her tear it open and he held his breath.

There was a little silence as his mum read the letter. Then she said, "Oh, how nice!"

What? Jason blinked. It was a nice letter? He went into the hall and there was his mum with a big smile on her face.

"Did you know about this?" she said. "Did your friend say her mother was going to ask you to tea?"

"My – friend?" Jason said.

His mum nodded. "Millie. She *is* your friend, isn't she?"

"I – um – suppose so," Jason said.

His mum held out the letter. "Look," she said. It was from Millie's mum and it said:

We are glad Millie has made such a good friend in her first week at her new school. Please can Jason come to tea on Friday? We will fetch them from school and drive Jason home after tea.

"Look at the address," Jason's mum said. "They live in that farm on the edge of town." She sounded very excited. "And there's the phone number. I'll ring right away, to say you're coming."

"No," Jason said. "I don't want –"

But his mum wasn't listening. She was on the phone already. "That's really kind of you," she said. "Jason would love to come. I'm so glad he's got a friend."

Jason stared at his mum as she made the phone call. It was too late to say no. His mum had said he was going – and she would make sure he did. Tomorrow he would have to leave school with Millie.

And everyone would laugh at him.

Chapter 5
Millie's Secret

Jason didn't want to go to school the next day. But it was Friday, the day his mum started work late. She always took him to school in the car on Fridays.

So there was no escape.

All the way there, his mum asked questions about Millie. And when they reached the school, she stopped right outside and peered through the car window.

"So which one is Millie?" she said.

Jason looked across the playground. "Over there," he muttered. "The girl with red hair."

"The *little* one?" His mum sounded surprised. But then she nodded. "She looks nice and – er – quiet."

"She's very quiet," Jason muttered.

Quiet and dull, he thought. But he didn't say anything. Instead he opened the door and got out of the car as fast as he could.

"Have a lovely time!" his mum called after him. "At Millie's! See you this evening."

She drove off and Jason walked into the playground, making sure he didn't look at Millie. All the other girls started to whisper together when they saw him.

"Watch out – here's Jason!"

"Keep away from him, everyone!"

"Don't even LOOK at him!"

They all turned their backs on Jason. And so did Millie. But before she turned away, she gave him a small, secret smile. And Jason knew exactly what she meant.

We're going to give them a BIG surprise this afternoon.

*

When they came out of school at the end of the day, there was a dented old truck parked outside the main entrance. A big man with bright red hair was leaning against the side of the truck. When he saw Millie, he started to wave and yell.

"I'm over here, princess!" he shouted. "Where's your friend?"

Millie was standing next to Jason. "Come on," she whispered. "Time to surprise everyone."

She grabbed Jason's hand and pulled him across the playground. Millie's dad grinned and opened the door of the truck.

"Great to meet you, Jason!" he said. "Jump in!" Then he looked across the playground. "What's wrong with all those other kids?"

Jason turned round to see. Everyone in the playground was staring at the truck. They all had the same stunned look on their faces.

Millie laughed. "They're surprised," she said. "They didn't know Jason was my friend."

"Oh, Millie!" Her dad shook his head. "You love secrets, don't you?"

Millie nodded. Then she looked at Jason. "I've got another secret too," she said as they

climbed into the truck. "Bet you can't guess before we get to my house. I'll give you three guesses."

Jason tried to think of something weird. "You've – um – you've got fifteen pet snakes?"

Millie shook her head. "Wrong!"

Jason thought for a while. "You're a boxing champion?" he said at last.

Millie giggled. "No – but you're getting closer."

"She borrowed one of my boxing gloves the other day," her dad said.

Jason laughed. He couldn't imagine Millie in a boxing ring.

"Better think carefully," Millie said. "You've only got one more guess. And we're nearly there. Look."

She pointed ahead, towards a big grey house at the top of the hill. Jason looked – and his mouth fell open. In between them and the house was a long sloping field, full of big round things. Big round ORANGE things.

PUMPKINS!

There was a whole field of them, right next to Millie's house. And at the top of the field was a heap of pumpkins, stacked up in a pyramid.

Chapter 6
Tea and Pumpkins

Jason stared at the pumpkins. Was it possible? Could Millie – quiet little Millie – be the person behind the Pumpkin of Doom?

He was so surprised   and so angry – that he couldn't speak for a moment. He kept staring at the field as they drove past it and turned into the drive of Millie's house. Millie's dad stopped the truck and Millie jumped out.

"You've still got one more guess," she said to Jason.

Jason jumped out too. He was so angry that he wanted to thump Millie. But he couldn't. Not with her dad standing there.

"It was YOU," he shouted. "You did all those PUMPKIN things!"

He picked up a big stone from the side of the drive and threw it, as hard as he could, at the heap of pumpkins.

The stone hit the top pumpkin and set it wobbling. The pumpkin wobbled from side to side, faster and faster – and then rolled off the heap and went bouncing into the field and down the slope.

As it fell off, the pumpkins below it started to move too. And then the ones under them. All of a sudden, all the pumpkins were rolling off the heap and bouncing down the field, in a huge orange landslide of doom.

Millie's dad got out of the truck and frowned at Jason. "Why did you do that?"

Jason pointed at Millie. "She – she –" But he was too angry to speak.

"It's OK, Dad," Millie said quickly. "We'll get the pumpkins back. Come on, Jason." She ran to fetch a wheelbarrow from the shed beside the house and started to wheel it down to the bottom of the field.

Jason ran after her. "Why?" he said. "Why were you so mean to me?"

Millie kept walking along with the wheelbarrow. "*You* were mean to *me*," she said. "You pushed me over on my first day at school. And then you let me get into trouble for being late. And then –"

"And then what?" Jason said crossly.

Millie grinned. "Then I kept having new ideas for the Pumpkin of Doom. I was having too much fun to stop." She stopped the wheelbarrow and started to pick up the pumpkins and put them into it.

Jason didn't know what to do. He wanted to go home, but he could see that Millie's dad was watching them from the top of the field. Maybe he should help with the pumpkins first. He began to pick them up and put them in the barrow too.

They had to fill the barrow over and over again, wheel the pumpkins up to the house and then go back for more. It was hard work and they only just finished in time for tea. Jason was still angry, but he was very hungry too. *I'll stay for tea*, he thought. *Then I'm going straight home.*

"My mum's cooked a special pudding," Millie said as they emptied the barrow for the last time.

Jason reached up and put the last three pumpkins on top of the heap. *Very* carefully. "What kind of pudding?" he said.

Millie grinned. "Wait and see."

*

There was a huge salad first, full of eggs and tomatoes and lettuce. When they'd finished that, Millie jumped up.

"I'll get the pudding," she said.

She brought the pudding in. It was a big round tart with an orange filling – and Millie had propped a notice on top of it.

I AM THE PUMPKIN PIE OF DOOM

Millie's parents didn't understand. And Jason couldn't explain what the strange words meant. Nor could Millie. They were both laughing too much.

Our books are tested
for children and young people by
children and young people.

Thanks to everyone who consulted on
a manuscript for their time and effort in
helping us to make our books better
for our readers.